JAYDE PERKIN is a freelance artist whose clients have included Penguin Books and Germany's *Das Magazin*. She has written and drawn extensively about grief for all ages and won the East London Comics & Arts Festival x WeTransfer Award in 2018. Jayde lives in Bristol, UK. Visit her website at jaydeperkin.com or follow her on Instagram @jaydeperkin.

First published in the United States in 2020
by Eerdmans Books for Young Readers,
an imprint of Wm. B. Eerdmans Publishing Co.
Grand Rapids, Michigan

www.eerdmans.com/youngreaders

Original title: *Mum's Jumper*
Written and illustrated by Jayde Perkin
© Book Island, United Kingdom, 2019

Manufactured in China

29 28 27 26 25 24 23 22 21 20   1 2 3 4 5 6 7 8 9

Library of Congress Cataloging-in-Publication Data

Names: Perkin, Jayde, 1991- author, illustrator.
Title: Mom's sweater / Jayde Perkin.
Other titles: Mum's jumper
Description: Grand Rapids : Eerdmans Books for Young Readers, 2020. |
  Audience: Ages 4-8 | Summary: After the loss of her mother, a young girl
  and her dad find a new way to live with grief with the help of her mom's
  sweater.
Identifiers: LCCN 2019032514 | ISBN 9780802855442 (hardcover)
Subjects: CYAC: Grief—Fiction | Death—Fiction.
Classification: LCC PZ7.1.P447495 Mo 2020 | DDC [E]—dc23
LC record available at https://lccn.loc.gov/2019032514

mom's Sweater

Jayde Perkin

Eerdmans Books for Young Readers

Grand Rapids, Michigan

"Visiting hours are over," said the nurse.

"We love you,"
we told Mom.

We left the hospital, and I wished
that Mom could join us.

Her favorite flowers lined the streets.

The next morning,
the phone rang.

It was the
hospital.

"She's gone,"
they said.

"Gone where?"
I asked.

It didn't feel real.
Nobody pinched me.
But if they did,
I'm sure I wouldn't
have felt it.

It was cold. I felt tired.

But I couldn't sleep.

The next few weeks were blurry.
Many people brought us cards and flowers.

Everyone would say, "I'm so sorry."
But it wasn't their fault.

There was a funeral.
There were more flowers.
There were more "I'm sorry"s.

There were also sandwiches,
but nobody wanted to eat them.

A dark space began to follow me around.

I found it hard to concentrate at school.

The sounds and voices around me were distant and floaty.

My body ached, like I'd been swimming for days;
how could I get to the shore?

Dad told me this feeling is normal.

It's called grief. He was swimming too.
We were grieving together.

The teachers and my friends at school
were all really kind...

...so I couldn't understand
why I still felt so alone.

Sometimes I even felt angry that my friends had moms who picked them up from school.

Dad and I slowly began to sort through
Mom's things. Why would she leave
them all behind?

She loved this sweater.

I love it too.

It smells like her.

Over time
it began to smell
like me instead.

And later Dad put
it in the wash.

Some people say that grief gets smaller over time.

But Dad says it's a little more complicated than that.

Dad says the grief is like Mom's sweater.

The sweater stays the same size,
but I will eventually grow into it.

The grief may stay
the same size.

But my world will grow
bigger around it.

I, too,
will grow.

I put the sweater in a drawer.
I don't need to wear it every day.

But I like to know it's there.

I feel Mom everywhere.
She's in the ocean,
in the flowers,
and in me.